Chapter 1:

The Idea

Caroline's best summer started when she fell out of a lemon tree.

Caroline was helping her grandmother pick lemons to make lemonade. Caroline's grandmother made the sweetest lemonade in all of Rivertown. Nothing tasted better on a warm summer afternoon.

After Caroline picked all the lemons she could reach from the ground, she decided to climb the lemon tree to pick the juicy-looking lemons in the higher branches.

She shimmied onto a tall branch and stretched to reach the bright yellow lemons just waiting to be picked. But just as she started to reach them – CRAAACK!!

The tree branch holding Caroline suddenly snapped! Down she fell, along with the lemons.

Caroline landed in the soft grass under the tree and laid there feeling more embarrassed than hurt. She also felt sticky after several juicy lemons fell on her.

Caroline's grandmother saw the whole thing and rushed over. "Caroline! Are you okay?! Did you hurt yourself?" she asked.

"I . . . I think I'm okay," Caroline answered, still feeling dazed (and sticky).

Caroline's grandmother looked her over and saw some cuts and bruises. Being a grandmother, she didn't want to take any chances. "We'd better have the doctor take a look at you," she said.

They drove to Rivertown Hospital, where Dr. Wellesley examined her. "You'll be fine," he told Caroline as he cleaned her cuts and applied some bandages. "But you should try milk instead of lemonade for a while. Cows are much closer to the ground."

As Caroline got ready to go home, she saw her friend Shannon coming in for a check-up. Shannon had been very sick a few years ago, and ever since she needed to use a wheelchair. Shannon once told Caroline she would need her wheelchair for a long time.

But Caroline didn't recall Shannon's wheelchair like it was now. It was all scratched and tarnished, its seat worn and patched, and its wheels were missing several spokes. Worst of all, it wobbled and squeaked whenever it rolled.

"Shannon – what happened to your wheelchair?" Caroline asked. "It's just old," Shannon told her. "I've used it so much it's getting worn out, like an old pair of shoes. I need to get a new one, but the kind I need costs more money than my parents can afford to pay right now. So I'll just have to make do with this one."

All the way home, Caroline thought about her friend Shannon. If Shannon had to use a wheelchair, at least she should have one that doesn't wobble and squeak. Caroline wished there was something she could do to help her friend.

When they got home, Caroline's grandmother made her a glass of lemonade with the lemons they picked from the tree. "This will make you feel better," her grandmother told her (as grandmothers are known to do). Caroline savored the sweet lemonade and smacked her lips in delight. "Grammy," Caroline told her, "this lemonade is so good you should sell it!"

Just as she said those words, an idea as bright as the sunbeams on the river that afternoon popped into Caroline's head. What if she sold her grandmother's lemonade, and used the money to help Shannon buy a new wheelchair? She was sure people would line up on a warm summer day to buy a glass of her grandmother's cool, sweet lemonade – especially if they knew it would help Shannon!

Chapter 2:

The Ripple

The next day Caroline had her grandmother share her secret lemonade recipe and show her how to squeeze the lemons just right.

Then Caroline set up a stand at the end of her driveway and made a sign. She was so excited!

Caroline worked at her stand all day, squeezing lemons and pouring lemonade for people as they passed by. Mixing so much lemonade was hard work, but Caroline didn't mind – she was having so much fun making friends with each new customer.

At the end of the day, Caroline brushed off all the lemon peels stuck to her clothes and counted the money she had collected: 20 . . . 21 . . . 22 . . . 23 . . . 24 . . . 25 dollars! Caroline realized it may not be enough to buy Shannon a whole new wheelchair, but at least she could help Shannon a little bit – and she sure had fun doing so.

Among Caroline's first customers that day were her friends Lindsay and Griffin, who stopped for a glass of lemonade on their walk home from a swim in the river.

The two friends drank their lemonade and talked about how much fun Caroline was having at her lemonade stand. They also wanted to do something to help Shannon — they both knew how much her wheelchair wobbled and squeaked. But what could they do?

Suddenly, Lindsay had a thought! Her dad was always leaving spare change around the house – pennies under the sofa cushions, nickels in the car, even dimes in the dog's bed! Lindsay and her mom were always picking up her dad's coins. What if Lindsay and Griffin collected all the coins their parents didn't want and used them to help Shannon? They each thought this sounded like a marvelous idea and raced home.

Lindsay and Griffin first searched their homes for all the spare change they could find – they looked behind chairs, under rugs, even in the washing machine!

It was almost like a treasure hunt.

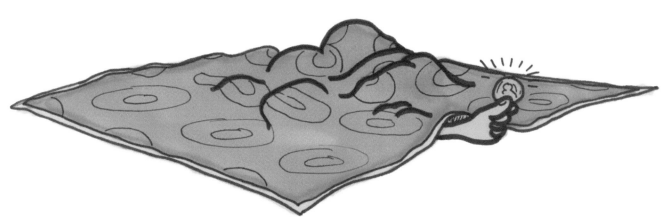

Next, they went door to door down their street asking their neighbors for any spare change. They said it was to help Shannon get a new wheelchair. Everyone was glad to help. Lindsay's neighbors Catherine and Katelyn even donated a whole jar filled with the coins their dad put in there each time he said a bad word. (He tended to say a lot of bad words each time he tried to fix things around the house.)

At the end of the day, Lindsay and Griffin emptied their bulging pockets and bags to count all the coins they had collected: 25 . . . 30 . . . 35 . . . 40 . . . 45 . . . 50 dollars! The two friends realized it may not be enough to buy Shannon a whole new wheelchair, but at least they could help Shannon a little bit – and they sure had fun doing so.

After Catherine and Katelyn donated their spare change to Griffin and Lindsay, they talked about how much fun their friends seemed to be having collecting coins. They also knew how much Shannon needed a new wheelchair. "It sure does wobble and squeak," said Catherine. They wished there was something more they could do to help.

Just then their dad came home from work. "Boy, Dad's car sure is muddy," said Katelyn. "I wouldn't be seen driving that car around Rivertown if you paid me!" "What if he did pay us – to clean it!" exclaimed her sister. "What do we look like . . . a car wash?" Katelyn asked her. "No," Catherine answered, "but we could start a car wash . . . and give the money to Shannon!"

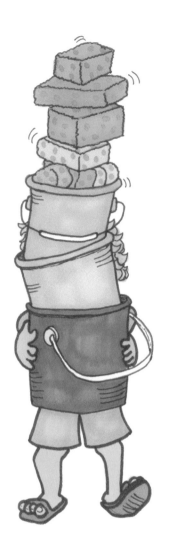

Catherine and Katelyn decided a car wash was a great idea. They collected all the buckets, sponges, and soap they could find.

Their friends Garrett and Charlie offered to help. They had an extra-long garden hose that was perfect for washing cars.

They all helped make signs for the car wash and hung them around the block.

All weekend the four friends washed cars: Catherine soaped them up, Katelyn rinsed them off, and Garrett and Charlie wiped them clean. They washed cars and trucks of all shapes and sizes. Caroline and her grandmother even stopped by in their muddy car. Washing cars was hard work, but the friends didn't mind. They were having so much fun seeing who could make each car the soapiest and launching sneak attacks with the hose when one of them wasn't looking.

At the end of the weekend, Catherine, Katelyn, Garrett and Charlie wiped the soap bubbles out of their hair and counted all the money they had earned from washing cars: 50 . . . 60 . . . 70 . . . . 80 . . . 90 . . . 100 dollars! The four friends realized it may not be enough to buy Shannon a whole new wheelchair, but at least they could help Shannon a little bit – and they sure had fun doing so.

Chapter 3:

The Paddle

Driving home, Caroline's grandmother liked how the car wash made her car look almost brand new. She also bought lemonade at Caroline's lemonade stand and donated her spare change to Lindsay and Griffin. She was proud of all the kids in Rivertown for working so hard to help their friend Shannon. She was also happy to see that they were having so much fun doing it. In fact, Caroline's grandmother was inspired! She thought that if all these kids can do something to help Shannon, why couldn't she?

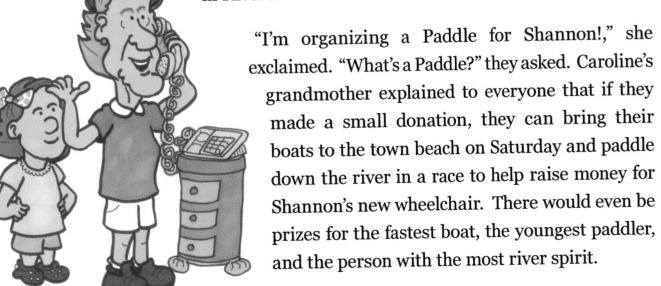

And she knew just what to do. As soon as they got home, Caroline's grandmother called all her friends and neighbors in Rivertown.

"I'm organizing a Paddle for Shannon!," she exclaimed. "What's a Paddle?" they asked. Caroline's grandmother explained to everyone that if they made a small donation, they can bring their boats to the town beach on Saturday and paddle down the river in a race to help raise money for Shannon's new wheelchair. There would even be prizes for the fastest boat, the youngest paddler, and the person with the most river spirit.

Everyone in Rivertown thought a Paddle to help Shannon was a wonderful idea. They were glad for any reason to be out on the water in the summer. The whole town looked forward to the big race.

When the day of the Paddle arrived, Caroline met her grandmother at the town beach. Caroline couldn't believe her eyes – for as far as she could see, the river was full of kayaks, skiffs, canoes, paddle boats, rafts, shells, and anything else that could be paddled down the river. Her friends Griffin and Lindsay were there, as well as Catherine, Katelyn, Garrett and Charlie. It seemed to Caroline that almost everyone in Rivertown was at the Paddle. Even Dr. Wellesley rode in the fire boat in case anyone needed help.

Caroline's grandmother stood on the beach ready to start the Paddle. "Because of all of you," she announced, "we have a special guest here today to help us start the Paddle!" She pointed toward the ramp at the end of the beach, and the crowd turned their heads to see who it could be. Just then Shannon appeared and glided down the ramp in a shiny new wheelchair! No more wobbles! No more squeaks! All of the money that had been collected from the lemonade stand, the coin collection, the car wash, and the Paddle was just enough to buy Shannon a new wheelchair.

Shannon rolled smoothly to the end of the ramp, with a huge smile on her face. The crowd burst into applause. The Rivertown cannon had been placed there, and Shannon pulled its cord. BOOOOOM went the cannon, signaling the start of the race.

Shannon did gleeful twists and turns in her new wheelchair, waving to everyone as they splashed by. As Caroline and her grandmother set off in their kayak, Caroline watched the water drip off the end of her paddle. When each drop hit the surface of the river, it made a small ripple in the water. That small ripple then made a slightly larger ripple, which then made an even wider ripple. Each ripple grew bigger and stretched farther than the last. Caroline realized the same thing happened in Rivertown that summer – first she opened her lemonade stand, and that inspired the coin collecting, which then led to the car wash, and now the Paddle. Each activity was bigger than the last, all of it was fun, and all of it did its part to help someone in need.

Caroline gazed at the long parade of boats paddling across the water under the shimmering sun. The whole town was having fun on the river that day. To think this all started with just a glass of lemonade!

Tips For Encouraging Your Child To Be Philanthropic

1. Identify a need. The recipient of your philanthropy could be a friend from school, someone you saw on the news or read about who needs help, or an organization in your community with a specific need (such as a church, school, or community center). It is important that the cause is meaningful to your child and to let your child choose the cause or recipient himself/herself.

2. Plan the event. Keep it simple and be creative! There are countless ways to give, and countless things to give – not only money, but also time, talents, donated items, and more. So use your imagination. Some tried and true ideas of fundraising activities for children of all ages include: a lemonade stand (or other food stand), car wash, coin drive, can drive, backyard carnival, race/walk/athletic contest, bake sale, toy drive, garage sale, clothes drive, and so many others.

3. Every little bit counts. Remember – even a little bit can help a lot. So don't let the amount you raise define success of the event. One dollar, ten dollars or one hundred dollars – it all adds up.

4. Have fun! Engage others in your event, including friends, family, neighbors, and classmates. It makes the effort more fun, spreads interest in the cause, and inspires others to be philanthropic. It's also a great socializing opportunity. By making philanthropy fun, children will become lifelong givers!

One hundred percent of the proceeds from the sale of this book go to the Foundation for Community Betterment. The Foundation for Community Betterment is a national non-profit organization founded in 2000 by a group of friends in their 30s seeking to "better" their communities by making an immediate, positive impact on the lives of needy individuals, families, or entire organizations who currently lack the means to succeed. In the last ten years, the Foundation for Community Betterment has distributed proceeds to over 150 individuals and organizations, both in the United States and abroad, with the goal that simple actions can create a ripple effect of goodness – when its recipients continue to positively impact those around them. For more information, please visit www.communitybetterment.org.

the foundation for
communitybetterment
a social network with a social conscience

CPSIA information can be obtained
at www.ICGtesting.com
Printed in the USA
246021LV00011B